INTO THE RED WASTES

The Burning Sands: Book Two

BY

B.K. Bass

Published in the U.S. by B.K. Bass, 2022

First Edition, 2022
Published by B.K. Bass in the United States of America

ISBN: 9798365985964

Cover art licensed from Dreamstime.com

B.K. Bass can be reached at https://bkbass.com/contact/

For the latest news, subscribe to B.K.'s newsletter here:
http://eepurl.com/dpaU6f

Visit the author's website at https://bkbass.com

Contents

Chapter One ... 1
Chapter Two ... 10
Chapter Three ... 19
Chapter Four ... 28
Chapter Five ... 39
Chapter Six ... 51
Chapter Seven ... 58
Chapter Eight ... 69
Chapter Nine ... 80
Chapter Ten ... 90
Chapter Eleven ... 103

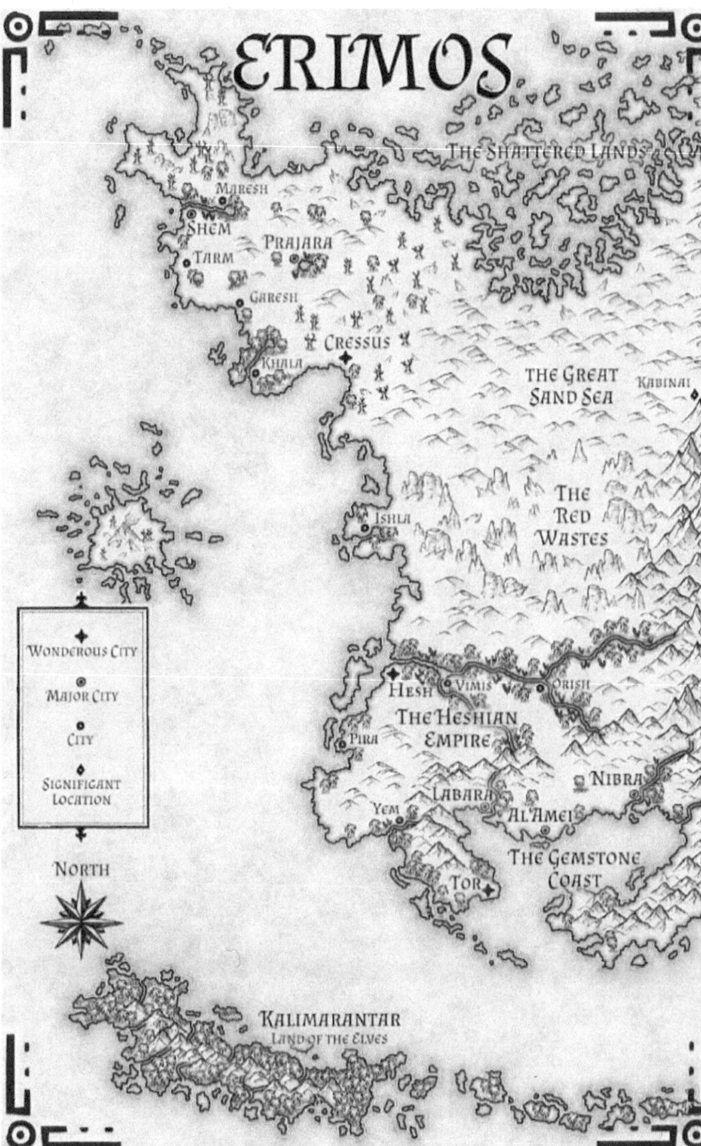
ERIMOS
THE SHATTERED LANDS
MARESH
SHEM
PRAJARA
TARM
GARESH
CRESSUS
KHALA
THE GREAT
SAND SEA
KABINAI
THE
RED
WASTES
ISHLA
WONDEROUS CITY
MAJOR CITY
CITY
SIGNIFICANT
LOCATION
HESH
VIMIS
ORISH
THE HESHIAN
EMPIRE
PIRA
NIBRA
LABARA
YEM
AL'AMEI
THE GEMSTONE
COAST
TOR
NORTH
KALIMARANTAR
LAND OF THE ELVES

INTO THE RED WASTES

Chapter One

The bow creaked as Brego drew back and took careful aim. Between strides of the horse below him, in a moment where he felt as if he could soar like the vultures overhead, Brego loosed the arrow. The projectile whistled through the air, spinning until it struck home, and the nomad's prey let out a shrill cry and slumped into the side of a dune. The shifting grains of the Great Sand Sea flowed over the still body.

Brego drew back on Pasha's reins and leaped from the horse as it slowed to a trot. He strode up the rise of the dune, his legs sinking further into the sand with each step. His quarry was buried by the time he reached it; only the black fletching of the arrow whipping in the wind betrayed its presence. The nomad sheathed the bow at his waist and reached into the soft sand. His fingers searched for a moment, then wrapped around a scaly hide. He pulled, drawing the yasalki's corpse back to the surface.

With a sharp jerk, Brego freed the arrow from the arm-length, copper-colored lizard, rubbed sand across the arrow to clean the blood from it, and slid it into the quiver on his hip. He tromped back through the sand to his waiting horse and added the yasalki to a brace of three others he felled earlier in the day.

The stallion whinnied and shook his head.

"I know, my friend," Brego said as he patted the horse's neck. "They stink, but we are done for the day." Brego grasped the saddle and pulled himself onto the dun-colored horse's back. As he settled himself, he gazed west over the tops of the dunes. Aporo, the larger of the world's two suns, was nearing the horizon. With Aporo's hunt almost done for the day, so too was Brego's. Night would soon fall, covering the desert in brief darkness before the next long day.

Brego pulled the cloth wrapping his face and head tighter, then gathered his cloak to shield himself from the blowing sand as he turned Pasha about. Squeezing the stallion with his knees and giving a soft click of the tongue, he urged his mount forward. Pasha stomped through the deep, shifting sands at first. As they left the massive dune behind, he found surer footing and sped to a canter.

Dunes surrounded them, so they kept to the narrow passages and harder ground between. Beyond those within sight, row upon row of the sand-swept rises loomed over the Great Sand Sea like bestilled waves. As Aporo slid below the horizon, the white sands took on an amber glow.

Before darkness enveloped the land, Brego returned to camp. Dozens of hide tents, ranging in color from tan to dark red, stood in concentric circles. Rooted by horse gut twine and ivory stakes, low to the ground and round with domed tops, they allowed the powerful desert winds to flow past. In the center of the camp, encircled by a central ring of tents, a large cookfire burned. It was sheltered by a small hearth of rough-cut sandstone that both shielded it from the wind and held the fire's heat in a small chamber for baking and roasting. Other fires burned in similar structures throughout the camp, and some inside the tents, but none were as large or as elaborate as the central fire. It was there that any member of the tribe might come to cook if they had not a fire of their own, or even eat if they had no food. Among the Taerwyn, none faced the night on an empty stomach. All the tribe possessed belonged to all the tribe.

The sight should have been familiar to Brego as he approached. He should have spent his entire life among his people, traveling the Great Sand Sea, surviving on the land, and trading with those who lived on its outskirts. Instead, he felt like a stranger among his own people. Brego passed more days in the quarries and fighting pits of Shem, a city of sparkling brass minarets far to the west and north, than he had in the Great Sand Sea. Taken when he was merely a child, he spent most of his life in chains. It was only recently that he broke his bonds and undertook the long, bloody trek back to his people.

Brego cast a glance skyward to find the moon rising

full overhead, casting a pale, silvery glow over the land. It had gone through three cycles since Brego rejoined his people, and still he wasn't sure if he would ever truly belong among them. This tribe wasn't even the one of his birth. The Taerwyn considered themselves one people—a massive family. Yet, there were dozens of small, wandering tribes that rarely, and only briefly, encountered one another.

Pasha stomped to a halt several yards from the fire, pulling Brego from his thoughts. The burly warrior swung his leg over and dismounted, then untied the brace of yasalki. He walked over to the cookfire, cutting one beast from the twine to keep and handing the other two to an older man tending the oven. The elder nodded and expressed his thanks. Brego returned the gesture with a forced smile, then strode toward his tent. Pasha followed him with no command.

All his life, Brego thought he would be at peace once he returned to his people. He would be free. In most ways, he was. However, something nagged at him. Something about life with the tribe didn't feel free. Roaming the desert, making their home where they found their feet, and living from the land and caring for it—all these things should make him feel free. Regardless, he felt nearly as confined as when bound with chains in the past. He was tied to the tribe, to duty, and to the whims of the desert. Brego was subservient to no man, yet he was bound to the tribe. He knew he should be thankful, but something inside him yearned to set out on his own. To forge his own path. To determine his own destiny. To answer to no man or woman.

Throwing back the flap of his tent, Brego bent low and stepped inside. In the center, he stood upright and removed his cloak and head wrap. He daubed sweat from his face and wiped the gleam of perspiration from his bronzed forearms before discarding the long length of cloth onto the pallet of hides that was his bed.

In the center of the tent, a small fire burned. Next to this sat a man with the ochre, reddish-brown skin of those who lived on the northern peninsula, west of the Great Sand Sea. Apa looked up and smiled. The curls of the Cressian's mustache wavered against his cheeks as he did. "You look hot, my friend. You spend too long out under the suns. Here, this will help." Apa held out a hand toward Brego, and another near the fire.

The air around Brego cooled as the magi drew warmth from it, and the fire crackled and roared to life as he fed heat into the coals. Magi were rare in any land and possessed strange gifts. Apa's gift was the ability to manipulate heat and fire. Brego had seen him throw handfuls of liquid flames at foes, blast them with sand born on gusts of hot air, and even form a giant monster of smoke and ash. But it was these subtle, delicate acts that amazed Brego the most, no matter how many times he witnessed them.

"As if it were not hot enough in here already," a coarse, low voice—sounding like a gnashing of stones—grumbled from across the tent. Khag lay on his side on another pallet, an open book appearing tiny in his large hands. The red-skinned orc would stand a head taller than Brego, could he stand upright in the low tent, and was two spans wider at the shoulder. He wore only simple trousers of black orgok wool. The firelight danced across his bare crimson chest and seemed to sparkle in the white tattoos that covered him from cheek to foot.

"Quit your bellyaching, Khag," Apa said. "Can you not see our friend bears a gift? Why not put your culinary artistry to use and prepare us a feast?"

"Humph," Khag snorted. He set his book down and rose to his knees before the fire, reaching out a hand to accept the yasalki as Brego offered it forth. He scowled, his low brow knitting over his small black eyes. His lip pulled back in a sneer, exposing a long, sharp tusk jutting upward from one corner of his jaw and the broken stub of another opposite it. "More like a snack. Would that I were back in my kitchen in Khala, I could perform miracles. But this..." He trailed off, waving a hand at the simple fire and shaking his head. Without further complaint, the burly orc set to cleaning the yasalki, removing its guts and head, then ran a spit through the beast and set it over the fire.

Brego could not help but smile at the exchange as he sat down and removed his leather boots. While he felt little bond with his tribe, those actually of his blood, he was joined to these two by a different sort of blood. Brego, Apa, and Khag had fought, bled, and shed tears together. Men hunted them across the Cressian badlands as they attempted to help Brego flee his past. Captured, they shared bonds of iron and faced the arena of Cressus together, then escaped. However, they lost a brother in the process: Mashim, an eccentric Khalasian merchant and Khag's former employer.

Apa was the first to show Brego kindness, removing his shackles and granting him the choice to discover his own purpose. Khag was the first to show him the respect of a fellow warrior, fighting by his side simply because it was the right thing to do. For these reasons and more, Brego felt more at home with this man of the northern cities and this orc of the Red Wastes than he did with his own people.

Chapter Two

The nightmares came to Brego as they did most nights: a disjointed collage of a horror-filled past. Iron shackles and chains bound the images. Blood and sweat ran between them. The edges of each memory blurred and flowed together, with a current of pain and despair flowing beneath them.

Brego hauled stones cut from the quarries of Maresh. Blood flowed from his shoulder as ropes cut into his flesh across the long trek to Shem. There, legions of slaves raised the stones to construct towering edifices that lorded over the city as the masters lorded over their servants. Towering marble statues of more fortunate men, gilded with brass, gazed out over the city. Their unseeing eyes looked upon all who huddled in the city's cages as a reminder that none could escape the reach of their overlords.

Bronze blades bit into Brego's sunbaked flesh, leaving a latticework of scars that traced the tale of years spent in the fighting pits. Craven men who dared not set foot upon those sands leered and shouted from above, leaning over the precipice with wine and bread in hand. Only a narrow stone railing and the happenstance of their birth separated them from the chattel who fought for their very survival six feet below.

Men cried out in pain and terror as Brego buried his blades in their flesh. Torchlight flickered in subterranean halls, barely sufficient to chase away the shadows as he raced toward freedom. For every man or woman fleeing by his side, another two lay cut down by the guards. However, they would all find their freedom that night, either in escape or death.

Screams of battle filled the air. Beasts grunted, snorted, and sniffed as they sought their prey. Shouts of alarm rang out, desperate to raise the sleeping from their rest so they might defend the tribe.

This wasn't a memory. This was something unfamiliar.

The pain of the past gave way to the fear of the present.

Brego's eyes shot open to the sounds of frantic screams and shouts of anger. Nearby, Apa and Khag roused from their sleep. The fire in the center of the tent had burned down to smoldering coals, their red glow the only light in the darkness.

"What in the seven hells…?" Apa began, then trailed off as his eyes grew wide. He waved a hand through the air and gestured at the dwindling coals. They grew brighter, granting some light for the three to see by.

"Battle," Khag grunted as he rose and drew his heavy bronze scimitar from below his pallet. He paused and sniffed, his broad nose wrinkling and nostrils flaring as he drew in deep breaths. "I smell skisnik."

Brego's urgency neared panic at the mention of the ravenous, hound-sized lizards known to prowl the

Red Wastes and often used in hunting packs by the red orcs who lived there.

"This far north?" Apa asked.

"We should not be far from the wastes." Khag stopped by the flap of the tent and turned back. "Just pray it's only a stray pack of the beasts and not heralds of worse." With that, he threw the flap open and strode into the night.

Brego pulled on sand-colored linen pants and grabbed his sword—a slender, curved iron shamshir—before following the orc. Apa was on his heels by the time he exited the tent. While the magi was empty-handed, Brego knew he was far from unarmed.

The scene that greeted them as they left the tent was unlike anything they could have expected. It was more horrifying than even Brego's dreams. Flames lit the night as tents burned. Horses screamed as they reared from the fires and galloped away, their eyes rolling in terror. Some women ran after the horses, children wrapped in their arms, while others ran toward the screams with bow or blade in hand. Men yelled to rouse any who still slept and likewise charged toward the center of the camp.

Khag stood nearby, the glow of the blaze illuminating his red flesh. Before him stood what could have been his reflection. He faced another orc—red-skinned, bulging with muscles, and covered in white tattoos. The foe held a large, bone-handled axe with a jagged obsidian blade. Khag swung his heavy, two-handed scimitar around in a wide arc, batting the axe aside. He followed this by slamming the pommel of his weapon into his foe's face, driving the orc back in a daze, then swung his blade back around to open a bloody gash in his belly.

"What in the blazes is going on?" Apa cried out. He glanced from one side to another, seeming to focus on the fires blazing around them.

Khag turned his blade down and thrust it into the felled orc's chest, then looked back. "The Grashni are attacking."

"Perhaps we've wandered too close to the wastes," Apa offered.

"That can't be," Brego growled as he strode past. He marched toward the heart of the camp, where the sounds of battle were the loudest. "We're several days' ride from the wastes. My people know to give them space."

"I know this as well as you," Khag said as he fell into step beside Brego. "We've had peace for centuries, you in the sands and we among the stones. There must be some reason for this."

Apa followed behind them, his arms held out at his sides. "We can worry about the reason later. For now, we must focus on saving who we can." The flames engulfing the surrounding tents fizzled and shrunk as he passed. As they marched on, his hands and forearms glowed red, then orange, then white hot. The sleeves of his robes flared, blackened, and blew away as ash on the wind.

Another orc charged out of the darkness, larger than Khag and wielding a massive bone club festooned with obsidian shards. Brego ducked under a wide swing of the wicked weapon and rolled behind the orc. Khag met the enemy's backhand swing with his sword. The weapons met with a clash. Khag's muscles bulged as he pressed the foe back. Brego rose behind the orc and slashed out with the shamshir. The curved blade slid across the back of the orc's knees in a spray of blood, and he fell screaming. Khag brought his heavy scimitar down on the warrior's neck, silencing his cries.

The three raced toward the center of the camp. As they neared, a swirl of blades and bodies greeted them. Over two dozen red-skinned orcs marauded through the camp. More than twice that number of Taerwyn warriors had risen to meet them, and they were engaged in a bloody melee. Shouts of anger and cries of pain formed a chorus backed by the rhythm of weapons clashing. Ravaging through all this with gnashing, snapping jaws, the skisnik hunting beasts of the orcs lent their reptilian fury to the chaos.

"Apa," Brego asked, "can you do anything to end this?"

The magi shook his head. "I can't unleash the flames without fear of striking down your people as well. We will have to do this the old-fashioned way."

With that, Apa charged toward the nearest orc, his glowing fists held before him. He landed blow after blow on the enemy, each raining sparks and leaving scorched burns on the orc's flesh. Brego and Khag followed, diving into the battle and wading through the attackers. More Taerwyn joined them, and soon the press of human defenders nearly consumed the orcish raiding party.

A horn blew somewhere in the darkness. The orcs all turned at this, fleeing when they could break free. A few were cut down as they ran, but most of them escaped to disappear into the darkness of the desert. Soon, the chaos was over and the camp left to the Taerwyn.

Brego stumbled to the central hearth and dropped to his knees. Dozens of cuts and angry bruises covered his body, but his injuries were minor. He looked out over the twisted bodies filling the spaces between the burning tents with tears in his eyes. Apa joined him, the glow of his fists exhausted. Khag stomped between the flaming tents and peered out into the darkness of the night, seemingly ensuring no foes remained.

Over the moans of the injured and sobs of those who had lost loved ones, a voice cried out, "Timik!"

Brego's eyes shot up and he looked about, searching for the source of the call. He recognized that voice as belonging to Raniq, the tribe's chieftain.

"Timik, where are you?" he called out again.

"Raniq," another member of the tribe yelled. A

young warrior ran past Brego, blood streaming from a large gash across his shoulder and his arm hanging limply at his side. "I saw him."

Apa slumped down to the sand next to Brego and rubbed a hand across his weary face. "This bodes ill for the chieftain, my friend."

Brego nodded.

Raniq stepped out from a large tent across from the central hearth, panic in his eyes. He rushed over to the wounded warrior and grabbed his good shoulder. "Where? Where is my boy?"

The younger man cast his eyes down, unable to meet the chieftain's eyes. "They took him, Raniq. The red orcs took your son."

Chapter Three

The twin rise of the suns, Ora and Aporo, brought only more grief. As they cast their light down upon the ruined encampment, they revealed just how badly the Taerwyn had suffered through the night. For every tent still standing, another three were burned to ash. Even more were destroyed on the southern side of the encampment, along the edge where the orcs breached the perimeter.

Blood stained the sands among the ashes—of human and orc alike. Bodies lay strewn about. There were ten dead orcs, and over twice as many Taerwyn. Beyond those felled in battle, several men, women, and children—who were unable to escape the sudden blazes—lay charred within the burned tents.

Brego sat next to the central hearth in a daze. He fled a life of pain and death in search of peace, only for such chaos to be thrust upon him once again. Apa milled among the survivors, searching for those with wounds in need of tending and lending aid where he could. Khag stood at the edge of the central ring, a silent, crimson monolith daring to say or do nothing in the aftermath of a battle with those who all too painfully resembled himself.

Raniq kneeled in the center of it all, wailing in grief at the loss of his son, Timik. The injured young warrior sat nearby, recounting the tale of the boy's abduction as a woman dressed his wounded shoulder.

"I first knew he was in danger when I heard his cries. The boy shouted out in not fear, but defiance. I tried to run to him, but so many orcs stood in my way that I could not reach him. Two others must have heard the same, Nesher and Haldip, for they seemed to fight with the same urgency to reach your tent. We battled through the orcs, but they soon fell to the brutes. However, they purchased a path through the chaos with their deaths, and I could finally hear the cries of the boy.

"A hulking orc emerged from your tent, flanked by a pair of skisnik. He was taller and wider than even their largest warrior. He bore only one eye, the other covered with a bronze plate. In his arms, he clutched Timik. The boy screamed and fought. He kicked and struggled. Despite this, he could not break free. I charged the brute, but another orc lashed out at me as I neared. Its obsidian blade bit into my shoulder…"

He nodded at his wound as the woman wrapped it in bandages. "The blow twisted me about and sent me sprawling to the sands. Stars burst in my eyes. By the time I shook my head clear and looked up, that wicked horn blew, and the giant brute ran from the camp, Timik still held in his arms."

Raniq looked up, blinking away tears of pain and rage. "They took my son?"

The wounded soldier nodded, silent under his chieftain's gaze.

Raniq's head shot back and forth as he seemed to

search the camp. Brego thought at first he sought some clue, but it soon became apparent he was searching for something to lash out at. Or someone.

"You!" Raniq called. He rose to his feet, grabbed a fallen spear from the sand, and strode across the central ring.

Khag stood silent and still, his hands empty and hanging limp at his sides as the chieftain advanced upon him.

Brego shot to his feet and ran after Raniq. "Apa," he called out. "Apa, we need you!"

Nearby, the magi rose from tending the wounded and raced to Brego's side.

Raniq held the spear out and jabbed it at the red orc's throat, stopping only inches short of skewering Brego's friend, who did not flinch. "You! You brought this down upon us. You sent for them, didn't you?"

"No," Khag said, his voice calm.

"Confess!" Raniq screamed. "Confess, and your death will be quick. Refuse, and I swear by the spirits of my ancestors, I will make you suffer pain such as that only spoken of in myths."

"I had nothing to do with this," Khag said. His tone

remained steady, but his hands trembled. Brego could not tell what was boiling beneath the surface. Did his friend tremble with fear or rage? In either case, it was astounding he remained so calm.

Brego did not.

"Raniq!" he called out. "Do not threaten my brother. My hrashim!"

The chieftain turned to Brego, but the point of his spear remained at Khag's neck. "You would choose this beast as hrashim over your own people?"

The word was a sacred concept among the nomads. People who rested their heads wherever they found themselves had no name for home. People who relied upon the entire tribe working together for survival in the harsh desert of the Great Sand Sea had a different idea of family than most. Hrashim meant both home and family. It was the tribe itself. It was a bond of trust, loyalty, and service. It was the unity that ensured the survival of the Taerwyn.

"Yes," Brego said. "I told you when you found us in the desert. Where they go, I go. Where I go, they go. Khag and Apa are my hrashim. Threaten one of them, and you threaten me. If you wish to fight one of us, you fight all three of us."

Apa stood beside Brego, tall and proud. He made no move against Raniq, but neither did he try to calm his friend. His hands were at his sides, but were splayed wide, ready to absorb the heat of the surrounding desert should the confrontation come to blows.

A crowd had gathered at this point. Red-eyed survivors and bloody, injured warriors stood in a circle around the four men. Cries went up from the crowd, all of them filled with rage.

"Where is the boy?"

"He brought them."

"Make him talk."

"Blood for blood."

"Kill the beast."

"Kill all three of them!"

Brego kept his eyes locked on Raniq's, but spoke loud enough for all to hear. "Shame! You *all* should feel shame. How many times has Khag proved himself loyal to the tribe? Which of your tents has he raised? Who among you has eaten meat he hunted? What of the beasts has he defended the tribe from, and the stories has he told your children? How many of them has he taught to read? And now, you turn on him simply because he is an orc? Simply because he looks like the others who attacked us? Is this the Taerwyn way? To take in others when it serves you, only to cast rage upon them when you fear them?"

Raniq turned his attention back to Khag, jabbing the spear closer to the orc's throat. "His people attacked us. They took my son."

Brego stepped forward and laid a hand on Raniq's shoulder. "And he should be blamed for this simply because he was born among them? He hasn't walked with his kind in many years. When I was a boy, I was taken as a slave simply because I was born Taerwyn. I did no wrong. I did nothing to deserve a life of servitude and pain. The men of the west view us as less than them because we do not cower behind walls from the desert. And simply for this, simply for being born among my people, they saw me as nothing more than chattel to be used as they wish. Will you now turn upon Khag for the same reasons? Are we no better than other men?"

The cries from the assembled nomads died to a dull

rumble as the tribe murmured among themselves. Some mumbles of anger persisted, but they were few and faint.

Raniq's shoulders slumped as he lowered the spear. He looked up at Khag, who still stood motionless. Their eyes met and lingered, as if each were taking the measure of the other. Finally, the red orc broke the silence. "I mourn the loss of your people, all of whom I consider friends. I grieve the loss of your son, who I love as if he were of my own blood. I swear to you, Raniq of the Taerwyn, I had no part to play in this tragedy."

The chieftain's mask of rage melted under an onslaught of sorrow. His shoulders heaved as sobs wracked his body. "My son," he cried. "What have they done with my son?"

Brego opened his mouth to answer, but Apa grabbed his arm and gave a sharp tug. The nomad looked back and the magi, who shook his head.

Instead, Khag answered the chieftain. "I do not know where they have taken him or what they plan for him, Chieftain Raniq." The orc took a knee, lowering himself to below the Taerwyn's height. "But I swear on my honor that I will do all I can to find your son and return him to you."

Chapter Four

Toil and sorrow filled the day. The survivors gathered the bodies of the fallen and wrapped them in shrouds, then packed sand from where each fell into the wrappings to insulate the bodies from the harsh suns. The salt in the sand would help preserve the flesh for their journey. Normally, the Taerwyn laid their dead to rest wherever the tribe found itself, returned in death to the desert which sustained them in life. However, those who fell in battle and great leaders were taken to

Kabinai. Deep in the Great Sand Sea, the sacred Taerwyn necropolis was a hallowed resting place. The only city the nomads ever built was home only to the fallen heroes of the tribes.

Men cleared two sand sleds of goods to make space for the bodies, and still they were both overfilled by the time the grisly work was done. Teary eyed women laid hastily woven wreathes of desert herbs atop them. Legends said they would bless the spirits of the fallen in their journey through the spirit sands of the afterlife. In practice, they helped obscure the odors of the bodies as they made the long, hot journey to their final resting place.

Khag took it upon himself to deal with the bodies of the fallen orcs. Many among the tribe wished to leave them where they lay for the carrion of the desert to dispose of, but the red orc insisted otherwise. Despite their actions, he argued, it was only right to aid their passage to the afterlife as well. Customs among the Grashni, the orcs of the Red Wastes, differed from those of the Taerwyn. Fortunately for Khag, they were quite simpler. He hauled the bodies away from the camp and laid them out in a single line, ensuring each gripped a weapon in his or her hands. The dead would need them in Ushtok, the orcish underworld, where the Grashni believed their fallen kin fought an eternal war against forces of darkness to protect life and light from being extinguished across the world.

Sending them along their journey proved far easier than readying them for it. Exhausted, Khag slumped to the sands as Apa took over for him. The magi held his hands skyward, drawing in the warmth of the twin suns high overhead, then turned this on the bodies, engulfing each in flames. Soon, the wind would blow their ashes away, carrying their spirits to Ushtok.

With the dead cared for, the survivors worked on packing up what remained of their belongings. A small contingent would escort the dead to Kabinai. The rest gathered around Raniq, who sat astride a white gelding.

Brego, having gathered his belongings for the coming journey and finding Pasha among the chaos, approached the chieftain. "What is your intent?"

Raniq stared at Brego, the fire in his eyes matched only by the amber glare of Aporo as he approached the horizon behind the chieftain. Ora, still high overhead, lit the assembly in harsh white light. "We will pursue the red orcs and hunt them down to the last living soul. If my son remains alive, we will retrieve him. If he is dead, we will take him to Kabinai to rest with his ancestors. Either way, the orcs will pay in blood for what they have done—every one of them."

Apa and Khag approached at this. Both remained silent, but their worried expressions spoke more than words ever could.

Brego shook his head. "To blame all the Grashni for the actions of a handful is wrong, my chieftain."

Raniq sawed the reins of his horse, pulling the animal about in a tight circle. It neighed in protest at the harsh treatment and tossed its head. The chieftain leaned close to Brego. His eyes were wide and wild, and his bronze flesh flushed red with anger. "And what would you have me do? Were I to forgive such a trespass, would I not only be inviting more of the same?"

Apa stepped next to Brego, laying a hand on the bristling warrior's leg to calm him. "My friend does not counsel forgiveness, only moderation. It was not *all* the Grashni who attacked, but only a raiding party. We know not if they acted upon orders or of their own volition. Let us learn more before acting. You would not invite war upon your people if unnecessary."

Raniq stiffened further. "Do not deem to tell me what I would or would not do, nor dictate what is best for the Taerwyn, outsider."

Brego slid free of Apa's grasp as he sidled his mount closer to Raniq. "This *outsider* is my hrashim, lest you forget. If you shun him, you shun me. Apa speaks wisely, as he always does. You have oft heeded his counsel. Do so again today. Let there not be more bloodshed than necessary."

Raniq squinted at Brego, but his posture relaxed. "And what, exactly, do you suggest we do?"

Khag stepped forward, standing taller even than Raniq's horse, yet still looking up at the mounted chieftain. "I swore to you upon the twin rise of the suns that I would endeavor to find your son, and I stand by that oath. We do not suggest you abandon the pursuit of the raiders. Allow the three of us to scout ahead. Give us time to determine what is happening and attempt to rescue your son. If you march the tribe into the Red Wastes, rest assured that your hunt will become a war between the Grashni and *all* the Taerwyn. The Great Sand Sea will run red with blood from both sides. Is this what you wish?"

Apa chimed in. "He is right. With such small numbers, and with a Khag among us, they will not see us as so much a threat. And being of three peoples—Grashni, Taerwyn, and Cressian—we are less likely to be perceived as a political affront to the orcish dominion over the Red Wastes."

Raniq looked back to Brego. "You would do this? You would risk your life to aid this orc in finding my son and returning him to me?"

Brego nodded.

"And what of those who took him?" Raniq gripped the hilt of his sword. "What will become of them?"

"My chieftain," Brego said, "we will climb that dune when we come to it."

*   *   *

With little further deliberation, they agreed that Brego, Khag, and Apa would advance ahead of the tribe. Raniq seemed hopeful about their success, but anticipated their failure as well. The chieftain also knew he could not go to war with a meager handful of warriors. He sent swift riders out in every direction, hoping they would chance upon other Taerwyn tribes nearby. The tale of the orcish attack and the loss of a chieftain's son would be enough to draw more warriors to the cause, and soon Raniq's war band would swell with warriors ready to invade the Red Wastes. It would take several days for the messengers to gather reinforcements, and more for the warriors to assemble and travel south into the rocky domain of the orcs. After six nights, should Brego and his brothers fail their mission, there would be war with the orcs.

They set out without delay. Brego sat astride Pasha. The dun-colored stallion's black mane and tail stood out in the desert while his tan coat blended with the sands. The tribe gave Apa a piebald mare named Hesbeth from what remained of the tribe's stock. Her pristine white forequarters shone under Ora's blinding light, while her dark brown muzzle and hindquarters seemed to absorb the rays. Khag strode before them afoot, as always, having neither need nor desire to ride. Regardless, with his bulk, he would have been hard pressed to find a suitable mount among the tribe's stock.

They headed out under the harsh light of Ora, until she set and Aporo rose for his slow, lonely hunt across the sky for his swifter mate. The day cooled under the twelve hours of his amber glow, until finally he rested and the long day gave way to the brief night.

The three hunters had no hope of tracking their quarry in the darkness, so they made camp. As Apa built a small fire, Khag set about peeling a handful of small, round cacti to roast over the flames. They sipped at water skins from their saddles, fully aware it may be days before they find another source of the life-giving fluid.

Apa was the first to break the silence. "Why would they take the boy and no others?"

Brego shook his head as he sat by the fire. "If they were taking slaves, they would have taken heartier stock, and more than one. It makes little sense.

"Khag," the magi said, "surely you might have some insight into this mystery."

The red orc skewered a peeled cactus on a bronze dagger and held it over the fire. "I wish I had answers for you both, and for Raniq, but this behavior puzzles me as much as any of you. Timik is young and—apologies—physically unremarkable. He is no stronger than any other lad in the tribe. While an easy target, he seems hardly worthwhile for the risk made and lives lost to abduct him."

Apa twisted his mustache with his free hand while he held his piece of cactus near the fire. "He seems to have been the goal of the raid. The orcs set to the heart of the camp with little diversion, and once they captured the boy, a horn blew their retreat. I think they came specifically for him."

Brego withdrew his charred cactus from the flames and blew on it to cool the flesh. "But, why? Why take the chieftain's son, if not to raise the ire of the tribe?"

"Perhaps," Apa said, "that was the point. Maybe the Grashni *hope* to provoke a war."

Khag shook his head. "Despite my people's reputation as warmongers, they are quite content with the peace that has persisted for so long. There is enough strife in the south protecting their borders from the advances of the Heshian Empire. They know that peace with the Taerwyn is a boon not to lightly abandon."

Apa checked his cactus and, seeming unhappy with its progress, gestured at the fire. The coals grew brighter, then the magi held the plant over them with a self-satisfied sigh. "Then it was merely a raiding party? Orcish bandits, or something of the sort?"

"I hoped that, at first," Khag said, "but the more I consider what happened, the more I realize it seemed too organized for that. Too deliberate. No, there must be a purpose to this abduction. The Grashni must have some justification for this brazen attack."

Around a mouthful of the succulent cactus meat, with juices dribbling down his chin, Brego mumbled, "There is never a justification for taking a child."

Khag winced, likely remembering Brego's own history of being abducted as a child and sold into slavery. "Apologies, my friend. I meant only that in their minds, my kin must believe there is a necessity behind the act. They would not frivolously provoke a war with their northern neighbors."

"I understand," Brego said. "Still, it burns in my heart to think of what the boy must be suffering. I cannot fathom a reason to inflict such agony upon any being, not to mention the misery Raniq and the rest of the tribe face."

The red orc nodded, then stared into the flames. "I agree, but I also know my people. They do not act without reason. While taking Timik is unconscionable, they must have some sort of plan for the boy."

Chapter Five

The rise of the twin suns soon arrived, and the trio stirred from their rest to continue the hunt. The windswept grains of the Great Sand Sea hampered their progress by covering most signs of disturbance. They proceeded south regardless, knowing the orcish raiders would head in that direction, toward their home in the Red Wastes.

As the suns rose high overhead and the heat of the day peaked, Khag halted and kneeled in the sand.

Worried something was amiss with his friend,

Brego walked Pasha alongside the red orc. "Is all well? Do you need to stop for a rest?"

Khag shook his head, his attention still focused on the sands below him. He moved a massive hand over the grains, his fingers splayed wide, and caressed the ground beneath him. "There are tracks under the sand. I can barely make out the impression, but it is deep." He ran a finger along a narrow line that barely caught a shadow under the blinding suns, and another, then a third. "Long talons under a great weight, and the size of the track is over three spans wide." He rose to his feet and took several steps to the side, careful not to disturb the already concealed tracks or the loose sand surrounding them. "Another here." He stepped forward and kneeled again. "And another."

Apa drew up beside Brego, wiping sweat from his brow with the loose end of the sash tied around his waist. "What could make tracks so deep the wind hasn't blown them over already?"

Brego looked back. The trail of hoofprints in the desert behind them was already difficult to discern as the shifting sands, born aloft on the hot wind, filled the impressions.

"Something very large," Khag said. "Khalati, if I'm not mistaken. At least one, if not more. The ground here is low, and the surrounding dunes protect it somewhat from the wind. If more traveled alongside, over the dunes, their tracks are lost to the desert."

Memories of the beasts ran through Brego's mind. He encountered such a monster once before, outside of Khala. The wild khalati was a massive, reddish-brown lizard with a maw capable of enveloping a horse. The beast remained docile, as they usually did in the wild, unless provoked or driven by hunger to attack. They typically made meals of orgok—large, wooly creatures whose herds populated the northern reaches, and which were often used by men as beasts of burden.

Not wanting to test the passive nature of such a gargantuan creature, Brego thought it best to avoid such an encounter. "We should divert our path, as not to become a meal for the monster."

"Nay," Khag shook his head. "We should follow the tracks as best we can. We are nearly upon our quarry, and this may be a sign of their passing."

Apa groaned and rubbed his sash across his face again. "Our friend may be right. I've heard tales of the

Grashni making mounts of the khalati. Wild tales of the giant lizards hauling massive wagons or rigged with howdahs to carry a dozen of the red orcs into battle."

"There's nothing wild about those tales," Khag said as he stood and turned back to the others. He walked up to Brego and Pasha to retrieve a waterskin from the horse's packs. "It is true. My people domesticate khalati for those purposes and more. It is likely the band we hunt kept the beast outside of the camp when they attacked, to keep it from danger or from causing more chaos. After they took Timik, they must have mounted the beast to make their escape. There's a good chance they may have drakes, as well."

Brego cocked his head to the side, unfamiliar with the term. "What is a drake?"

Khag sipped from the skin and flashed Brego a lopsided grin, made more comical by his one broken tusk. "Another reptile, closer to the size of a horse, common in the southern lands. They're a favorite mount in Hesh, where horses and orgok are rare. The Grashni raise them in the wastes as well. Some say they are descendants of stock taken from the Heshians themselves."

"Fantastic," Apa sighed. "Not only are the three of us racing towards a violent band of orcish warriors, but we're also going to be up against at least one khalati and possibly a bunch of drakes."

Khag returned the waterskin to the bundle of packs harnessed over Pasha's flanks. "Don't forget the skisnik."

* * *

As the day drew on, Aporo set, leaving Ora to crawl across the western sky alone. Then, after she set, Aporo rose again for his second race through the heavens for the day.

Throughout the day, the khalati prints became more readily visible. At first, Brego and Apa relied on Khag to track their foes. By the time Ora set, they could all make out the deep impressions of the giant lizards with ease. Alongside them, other tracks became visible. These smaller ones, Khag insisted, belonged to at least four drakes.

After nearly thirty-six hours under the scorching suns, the darkness of night descended once again.

While they were making progress catching up with their foes throughout the day, they did not wish to risk losing the trail at night. Also, none of them relished the thought of encountering the band of orcs while exhausted from the long day of travel. So, they made camp for the night and rested.

The three set out again just as the twin suns rose. The tracks were more obscured, but they were clearly much closer to their quarry than on the day before. In the distance, the ruddy plateaus, mesas, and buttes of the Red Wastes shimmered in waves of heat rising over the horizon.

As the deep, soft sand of the Great Sand Sea gradually gave way to the stony scrubland and sparse, spindly udai tree copses of the Red Wastes, silhouetted forms appeared on the horizon. By the time of Aporo's Hunt, the forms were more discernible. The lumbering khalati, with a massive, canopied howdah on its back, was plainly visible. Brego breathed a sigh of relief that there was only one of the beasts. Four orcs also rode atop drakes. Several others walked alongside, and small shadows darting between them were likely a pack of skisnik. Their quarry was finally within sight of the three hunters.

And they were within sight of their quarry.

A shrill cry rose, piercing the silence of the desert. The drake riders spun about at the call of the skisnik. Soon, guttural shouting joined the chorus. Half of the orcs marching on foot clambered atop the khalati, gaining a hold wherever they could as the massive beast was urged faster. The drake riders turned away and hurried along their path as well. Within moments, the mounted orcs fled into the distance, leaving six of their number behind.

These charged toward Brego and the others. More shrill cries filled the air as half a dozen skisnik charged ahead of them. Clawed feet dug gouges out of the coarse, rocky sands where the Great Sand Sea mingled with the stones of the Red Wastes as the reptiles closed on their prey.

"They send a rear guard to confront us," Apa said.

Brego shook his head in dismay. "I don't suppose they might be willing to talk."

Khag strode over and pulled his scimitar from Pasha's packs. "They have already made their decision. They have chosen blood." He then turned and raced toward the oncoming foe.

With a resigned sigh, Brego drew his bow from Pasha's other flank and dug his heels into the horse's ribs, urging his mount into a gallop. Beside him, Apa surged forward, a heavy, bronze-headed mace in hand. The riders overcame their orcish companion, but Khag's pace did not leave him far behind.

As the two forces closed the distance between each other, Brego loosed arrow after arrow. One, then two, then a third skisnik fell scrambling to the ground, shrieking in pain. Another arrow struck a charging orc in the throat. The hulking warrior dropped to his knees, clutching at his neck to staunch the blood flowing down his bare chest.

Apa, only a few paces ahead of Brego, was the first to meet the foe. He turned toward the side of the charging line and greeted the furthest orc to the left with the heavy bronze sphere of his mace. The Grashni's face exploded in a spray of blood and broken teeth before he collapsed, motionless.

Brego shifted his bow to his off hand and drew his long, curved sword. He slashed out to either side in fluid strokes, leaving two more felled orcs in his wake.

Before he could turn about for another charge, Pasha cried out in pain beneath him. Two of the remaining skisnik's jaws were locked around the horse's hind legs. Then, as soon as he realized what was happening, the world turned upside down.

Rough stone and sandy grit tore at his face and the heavy weight of Pasha rolled over his back. Brego rolled with the momentum of the fall, but the wind was knocked from his lungs. Panting, he grasped for his sword, but his fingers only found sand and loose gravel. Stars danced across a field of black before his eyes, and he realized he must have struck his head in the fall. Nearby, the hissing of the skisnik heralded his impending death.

Before their razor-sharp teeth sunk into his flesh, however, he heard the wet thunk of a blade biting through flesh of another sort and breaking bone. Then there was another, accompanied by an almost unnatural shriek of pain.

Blinking away the stars, Brego shielded his eyes from Aporo's harsh orange glow. A large hand of crimson flesh, bathed in the black blood of skisnik, reached out to him. "On your feet, friend. We are not done yet."

As Brego took Khag's hand and rose to his feet, the world swayed around him. He leaned on the orc's arm, sure it was only his friend's support that kept him from falling.

"Okay, *you* are done. Sit." Khag lowered Brego back to the stony ground, then took off at a sprint with his scimitar held over his shoulder, the bronze blade glinting in the sunlight.

In the distance, Apa swung his mace from atop his horse, fending off the thrusts of a spear-armed orc. The remaining skisnik snapped at Hesbeth's legs, only to be met by a kicking hoof. The reptile scurried away, blood running from broken fangs, but did not relent in its assault. It charged back in, leaping, and sunk its jaws into the tender flesh of the horse's throat. She screamed as she fell, tossing Apa to the rough, stony ground.

Khag charged at the other remaining orc, quickly dispatching him before rushing to his friend's aid. The skisnik bit and clawed at the dying horse, then fell under Khag's blade before it realized he was upon it. The last of the attackers halted his advance on the stunned Apa and spun around to hold Khag at bay with his long, obsidian-tipped spear.

"Hold!" Brego called out. "We need answers from this one." He struggled to his feet, again fighting against waves of dizziness, and stumbled toward the standoff.

"You will get no answers from me," the orc hissed as he jabbed his spear at Khag.

Apa rose while the orc's attention was on his kindred opponent and swung his mace in a lazy arc. The heavy bronze sphere thudded into the orc's back, forcing him off balance. As he lurched forward, Khag swung his scimitar around and knocked the spear from the orc's hands.

"You will yield, young one, or you will die." Khag stood hulking over the other orc, his own tattoos rivaling his foe's in both quantity and complexity.

Seeing the two face to face in the sudden moment of stillness, Brego realized the Grashni raider must have barely reached adulthood. Only a few white tattoos marked his shoulders and back. The markings told the story of a red orc's life and accomplishments, an intricate pattern that was added to over time. This young one's story seemed mostly unwritten. Khag's flesh, in comparison, was run through with intricate whorls and swirls from his forehead to his toes.

The younger orc fell to his knees, arms limp at his sides, and lowered his chin to his chest. "I yield."

Chapter Six

Pasha's cries of pain were soon silenced. Mauled by the skisnik, Brego knew the horse would never stand again. He kneeled beside his equine friend's body, tears of grief and rage running down his cheeks. He threw the blood-soaked knife with all his might into the rocky wastes and let out a cry of anguish that echoed from the distant plateaus.

Nearby, Apa and Khag bound their prisoner's hands with a length of rope.

"I would advise you to be cooperative," Khag said

in a hushed tone. "Our companion loved that horse. He is going to be in a foul mood."

"What does it matter?" the young Grashni asked. "You will kill me either way."

Apa cocked his head to the side. "We will? I rather expected we would let you live. We have no thirst for blood."

Brego rose from Pasha's side and joined the others, standing over the red orc, who sat surrounded by his fallen brethren.

"You drew it easily enough moments ago," the Grashni growled.

"When given no choice," Khag said. "We wished only to speak with the leader of your war band, not to attack. We will leave you to care for the fallen once we have answers from you."

The young orc pulled back his lips, revealing more of his small, sharp tusks. "Why are you traveling with these humans, dohathnik?" The last word dripped with scorn.

"Do-who?" Apa raised an eyebrow and shot a glance at Khag.

The older orc sighed and rubbed a large hand

across his face. "It means something akin to 'traitor' in the Grashni tongue."

Brego lashed out and struck the young orc across the face. "That is my brother you are insulting."

Khag grasped Brego's shoulder, stopping him as he was about to strike again. "Do not fret over it. Its meaning is more subtle than that. It can also simply describe one who walks with strangers. Like much of our language, subtle inflections impart the true meaning."

"I'm guessing from his tone," Apa said, "that's not what he meant."

The young orc rubbed the back of his hand across his mouth, and it came away stained with deep crimson blood. "Enough of this. If you have questions, ask them. Else, kill me and be done with it."

Brego crouched next to the orc, bringing him eye to eye with their captive. "Why did you attack our camp? Why take the boy?"

"Because of the prophecy. Our shaman bid us to prevent it from coming to fruition."

Khag took a step closer. "What prophecy?"

The prisoner sneered up at Khag in contempt. "When a dohathnik kneels to the sandwalkers, the worldbreaker will be found hiding as a child in the home of their chieftain."

"Sandwalkers?" Brego asked, looking up for an answer from Khag.

However, the red orc had turned and stomped away.

"Their word for the Taerwyn, I believe," Apa said.

Brego rose and followed Khag. "What's wrong?"

"Of all the half-witted…" Khag mumbled. His fists were balled at his sides, the muscles under the crimson skin of his thick arms and broad back rippling.

Brego stepped closer. "My friend, help us understand what is happening."

"Isn't it clear?" their orcish captive said through throaty laughter. "Your *friend* has bent his knee to your kind. To the sandwalkers."

Khag spun around, trembling with rage. "They think I'm the dohathnik from the prophecy because I've been living with the Taerwyn. Because of this, they think Timik is the worldbreaker. This is all my fault."

"Hold a moment," Apa said, still standing guard over the prisoner. "How could a Grashni simply living among the Taerwyn portent anything, let alone something that sounds so… dramatic?"

"Think about it…" Khag said as he strode back over to the prisoner's side. "My people and Brego's may have lived under a tenuous peace for nearly a century now, but both our histories are ones of conflict. The Grashni and the Taerwyn have warred on the borders of the Great Sand Sea and the Red Wastes for millennia. The common language of our peoples has always been that of blood and strife."

Apa shook his head. "That makes little sense. The Taerwyn are peaceful. Even the Grashni tend to keep to themselves."

"Peaceful," the prisoner huffed as he spat a mouthful of blood to the ground, a reminder of Brego's recent outburst.

Brego sighed and stood beside Khag, laying a hand on his larger friend's shoulder for reassurance as he explained to Apa, "I am pleased this is now our way, but shamed to say it was not always so. My people were once as savage and warlike as many believe the Grashni to be. They raided at the edges of the Sand Sea, terrorizing both human and orc alike."

"I'd heard stories," Apa said, "but always thought

prejudice shadowed them."

Khag rubbed his hand across his face in frustration. "No doubt they were exaggerated, from what I know of your northern kin. But in this tale, there is a grain of truth."

The prisoner rose to his knees and held out his bound hands. "While this is all very interesting, what of me? You have your answers."

"One more thing," Brego said as he strode over and pulled out the twin of the knife he'd ended Pasha's misery with. He held the slender, curved blade under the orc's throat. "Where are your people taking Timik? How do we find them?"

The red orc nodded toward the western horizon, as much as he could with a knife pressed at his throat. "Keep chasing the setting suns. You will see a tower of red stone surrounded by a plateau. My clan's home rests in an open chasm at its base. It is there they take the boy."

Khag stepped behind the captive, towering over him. "You would so readily reveal you clanhome?"

The smaller orc laughed. "What will the three of you do when you get there? You are no danger to an entire clan. You'll be feed for the khalati."

Apa grinned. "We may surprise you."

The prisoner glanced down at the blade still held at his throat, then met Brego's eyes. "Well?"

The Taerwyn lowered the blade. "What will they do to Timik?" he asked as he cut the prisoner's bonds.

The young orc smiled. "Your friend knows. Ask him."

Brego and Apa both looked up at Khag. The older orc trembled with rage, but drew in deep breaths, seemingly attempting to control his anger. "They will kill him under the light of the full moon.

"That's in three days," Apa said in a hushed tone.

Brego shook his head in dismay. "And Raniq will be here with his army in four."

Chapter Seven

After leaving the young orc to tend the dead, as promised, the trio pressed on afoot through the rest of the day, that night, and into the dawn. The suns rose overhead, casting light on the rocky scrubland of the Red Wastes. Russet towers, cliffs, and plateaus rose around them, obscuring the horizon in all directions save to the north, where the dunes of the Great Sand Sea were merely ripples in the hazy distance. Small lizards scurried away to hide as they stomped forward, urged beyond exhaustion by determination and the inexorable march of time. By midnight of the next day, Timik would be executed.

Khag sipped from a waterskin, then passed it to Brego. The Taerwyn pressed the mouth of it to his chapped lips and let a few drops coat his dry skin before running his tongue over it. Of the skins taken from the horses, it was the last one that still contained any moisture, and it was nearly empty. He passed it to Apa.

The Cressian shook the meager supply of water with a sorrowful frown before taking a sip. "Surely there is somewhere around here to find more. Khag, you were raised in these lands. Where do the Grashni find their water?"

The red orc shot the magi a sidelong glance, then averted his eyes before speaking. "You'd rather not know."

"I'd rather not die of thirst, is what I'd rather not," Apa said.

Khag sighed in defeat. "There are some springs along the feet of the plateaus, but they are rare and often well-guarded. The few of them which supply any ample amount of water are usually where my people make their homes. Should we find water, we will likely find a Grashni clanhome. Since it is the latter we seek, we shall probably find it before water."

Apa passed the waterskin back to Brego, who slung the deflated sack over his shoulder. "And what of their war bands, or patrols? What of those on the move, friend Khag? Where do they find water?"

"That, also," Khag said, "you would rather not know."

Brego's unyielding march faltered as he stepped closer to the red orc and laid a hand on his friend's arm. "If we did not want to know, we would not have asked. Tell us. It might save our lives."

Khag's lips parted in a rueful grin. His remaining tusk jutted out with what would have appeared as a snarl to anyone not familiar with the orc. "You might think as much, but no. With no water at hand, Grashni raiding parties find their moisture from the blood of the fallen. Beast, foe, and friend alike."

This was not an unfamiliar concept to Brego, who sustained himself for some time during his flight from captivity on horse's blood. This was a practice of last resort among the Taerwyn, reserved only for the most desperate of times.

"Wonderful," Apa muttered, throwing his hands up. He kicked a rock at a small, finger-sized lizard, who scurried into a thorny scrub for protection. It turned and glared at the magi as he passed. "So, all we need to do is catch a hundred of these tiny reptiles and drink their blood, and we might survive until dusk."

Brego stopped short and held his arms outstretched, signaling to the others to halt. "Or…" he said under his breath, "*one* of those."

Ahead, nearly hidden by a rocky outcrop, a single drake laid in the shade of the stones. Its long neck was curled over its back. Its head rested on a flank which rose and fell as it drew deep, even breaths.

The nomad drew his bow from its sheath on his belt and knocked an arrow. He took careful aim at the sleeping beast as Khag and Apa crept forward in silence. Brego took a deep breath, let it out, and loosed the arrow. The projectile whistled through the air as it flew, and the drake's yellow eyes snapped open. The beast swung its head around and rose as the arrow sunk into its shoulder—where only a moment before, its head had rested.

"Curse our luck," Apa yelled, hands outstretched. His clothes fluttered as warm air surged past him. Sweat beaded on his brow as a hot gust shot forth, filled with grit and sand, to buffet the rising drake. It stumbled as it turned to run, pressed against the stone wall it had sheltered beneath.

Khag charged at the struggling creature, scimitar in hand. The bronze blade flashed in the light of the suns as he swung it at the drake's neck, but the magical wind throwing the creature off balance also shoved the blade to the side. It came down against the stones, skittering in a rain of sparks.

The creature found its footing, took a moment to hiss at the red orc, and took flight.

"After it!" Brego yelled as he loosed a second arrow. It was tossed in the gale and sent skittering out of view. "Apa, enough with the wind."

The magi relaxed his arms and stumbled forward, heaving to catch his breath as the gust dissipated. "Apologies, my friend. It was the best I could think of in the moment."

"Apologize later," Khag roared as he found his footing and took off after the drake.

Brego followed just after.

"Go," Apa cried from behind. "The spell took much of the little energy I had left. Go!"

Khag turned the corner around a stone cliff. Brego nocked another arrow as he followed the orc into a narrow passage in the rust-colored stones. They ran for several minutes through the twists and turns of the narrow chasm. As the path grew into a maze of diverging crevices, a faint trail of blood droplets from the drake's wound was their only guide through the serpentine maze.

The red orc stopped at an intersection, studying the ground. "I think we've lost its trail."

Brego stepped forward and kneeled in the center of the narrow opening, scanning the red rocks and sand-blown grit for some sign of the beast's passing. He reached down and wiped away some of the grit, revealing a fresh gouge in a bit of sandstone, likely from a clawed toe.

Apa jogged into the opening behind them, sweat-covered, red-faced, and panting. "Well?"

"This way," Brego said, then took the lead through another narrow passage in the rocks.

The trail was barely wide enough for the drake to have passed through, but streaks of blood on one side of the passage confirmed Brego had chosen the correct path. The narrow gouge through the stones twisted and turned, and Brego could not see more than a few paces before him. In the distance, the scrambling of the drake's claws against sand and stone slowed to a halt.

"It stopped," Brego whispered over his shoulder. "Be ready."

With an arrow nocked and the bowstring drawn tight, Brego turned another bend in the path. The cliffs fell away to either side, then stretched on before rejoining each other, creating a round opening with paths opposite each other. In the center of this stood the wounded drake, surrounded by three others and a burly orc who was tending its wound. Another dozen orcs filled the open space, most of them with spears pointed at Brego's throat.

He drew up short and halted in his tracks, then Apa and Khag ran into him from behind.

"Oh, dear," Apa whispered.

"Well," Khag said as he laid his scimitar to the ground in defeat, "we found them."

*　　　*　　　*

The three hunters, stripped of their weapons and with their hands bound behind their backs, were led through the narrow passage opposite the small opening. This followed more twists and turns and met so many intersections of other paths that Brego would have struggled to remember the way on the best of days.

This was not the best of days.

One of the red orcs jabbed the butt of his spear into Brego's back as his pace faltered. He cast an angry glare over his shoulder, but picked up his pace, nonetheless. Other warriors separated him from Khag and Apa, eliminating any potential for whispered plans of escape. Though, that wasn't on Brego's mind in the moment. They had set out to find the orcs who took Timik, and they'd achieved that goal, although the circumstances were less than ideal. Still, every step, bound and captive or not, brought them closer to their objective.

Before long, the passage opened once more. To

either side, the tall cliffs stretched out to form the edge of a broad plateau, within the depths of which they had been traveling. Ahead rose a tall, narrow column of ocher stone that dwarfed the already imposing rise behind them, and beyond this the cliffs of the plateau circled around to form an enclosed space. Strewn between the monolithic structure and the broad cliffs were hundreds of ropes supporting canopies and awnings of cloth and reptile skins in a medley of reds, oranges, browns, and yellows. Beneath these, a network of raised platforms, ladders, and small buildings made of wood and bone clustered against the cliffs and the tower. From around their bases, structures of piled stones filled the space between them. In the small, round chasm, the canopies and awnings overhead sheltered the village from the suns.

More than a hundred scarlet-skinned orcs went about their daily lives—men, women, and children alike. Warriors sat hunched over obsidian axes, cleavers, and spears, grinding away at their edges with smooth chunks of granite. Some men hauled stone to reinforce their homes, while others lashed strands of animal gut around the trellises supporting the platforms against the cliffs. Women ground grains from desert scrubs in stone mortars, butchered game, or mended clothing. Young orcs, barely taller than Brego's hip, ran around the prisoners, jeering and laughing as their captors marched them through the village.

One of the orcish children, a slender boy whose tusks had barely grown past his lip, planted his feet before the nomad. He held a long, slender shaft of udai wood in his hands, sharpened at one end to create a rudimentary spear of his own. He cocked his head to the side and squinted, then asked, "Who are you? Do you want to play?"

The warriors escorting Brego and the others burst into laughter, and one of them kneeled before the boy and tousled his hair. The orc was larger than the rest, and the white tattoos covering his body nearly obscured his crimson skin. A shimmering bronze plate held in place by leather straps covered one of his eyes. Brego realized this must be the hulking orc described by the Taerwyn warrior back at their camp; the very one who fled with Timik in his arms.

The massive warrior's words and movements were

gentle, though. Those of a father, not a killer. "Not today, Thurog, my boy. Our..." He cast a glance over his shoulder at the three captives, then turned back to the child. "Our guests are on their way to see Chieftain Garnok. Maybe later."

"That's what momma said about the new boy when he got here," the child said, frowning in disappointment.

Timik is already here, Brego thought. *And this orcish child wanted to play with him?*

"Run along," the warrior said, rising to his feet and pushing the child to the side. "Go find some of your friends to play with. We have... *work* to attend to."

Chapter Eight

As they continued through the village, Brego looked up at the one-eyed orc marching beside him. "Do many of your clan know the northern tongue?"

The towering warrior harrumphed. "And this surprises you? You expected to find us grunting at each other like savages, I assume?"

Brego shook his head. "No, but your people and mine give one another a wide berth, and the city states of the peninsula are not welcoming of… *others*. This I know all too well from time spent in chains among them. I only wonder what opportunity you had to learn our tongue, and how many of you know it."

"Most of our young do. It is more difficult for those my age, but many of us have managed. Very few of our elders, aside from our chieftain, however, have learned."

"But, how? From whom?"

As they neared the tower of stone in the center of the village, the orc let out a rumbling chuckle. "Your clan is not the only one to take in strangers." He stopped, holding up a hand to halt the others. "Do your eyes fail you, human? Look around."

Brego did, taking a closer look at the clan going about their daily lives or gawking at the captives. As he peered into the village, he found an answer he had not expected. Among the red-skinned orcs, there were smaller forms bearing bronzed flesh not unlike his own. There, near a stone hut, a Taerwyn woman aided several Grashni matrons who were sewing hides into what would likely be another canopy overhead. Not far from them, a man who resembled Apa in many ways—who was most likely from one of the cities of the northern peninsula—worked at fletching arrows.

Another group of crimson-fleshed children ran by, with a human girl hot on their heels. Brego looked all around, and for every dozen orcs he saw, there was another human among them.

Apa seemed to have noticed this as well, as his eyes were wide. "Friend Khag," he said, "you never told us your kind lived with humans."

Khag appeared just as surprised. "I've been away from my clan for many years. They were fearful of humans then."

The large, one-eyed warrior nodded. "As well they may still be, brother. From what clan do you hail?"

"The Clan of the Sky Serpent," Khag replied, tilting his head back to reveal a tattoo resembling a coiled, winged serpent at the base of his throat.

The warrior nodded, and the bronze plate over his face glinted in the sunlight. "You are very far from home, then. I would doubt your clan enjoys such progress, being so close to the southlands. Our people still struggle against the humans there. Tell me: how did you come to be so far north?"

Khag let out a slow breath. "The story is a long and sad one. Let us simply say that my time among the humans was not always one of brotherhood. It was such until I was purchased by a man named Mashim, who freed me and became a good friend." Sorrow filled Khag's eyes at the mention of his lost companion.

Brego, too, felt the pain of loss at the merchant's name, so he sought to change the subject. "Where do they all come from? And how did they end up here?"

The large warrior glared down at Apa. "*Your* people are less welcoming to your own kind than we are to strangers." He waved a hand around at the people of the village. "Many of the humans you see among us are considered criminals by your kind or were taken from the sandwalkers as slaves. These lost souls escaped bondage and wandered into our lands, and here we gave them a home. Some of them have even started families among us, hence the young ones you have witnessed."

"Then, why take the boy?" Brego asked.

"The prophecy," Khag mumbled.

A strange look crossed the towering, one-eyed orc's face. Brego thought he saw sorrow there, or uncertainty, or perhaps regret. "Come," the orc said. "It seems you desire answers, and for that, you must speak with Chieftain Garnok. He will, I am sure, wish to speak with you as well."

They continued toward the pillar of stone in the center of the village. At its base stood a simple, round stone structure. It was larger than the others, but not by much. The only ornamentation that set it apart was a single hide banner hanging from a nearby post, which bore the image of a cliff sundered in two. Brego thought this might be the sigil of the clan.

The interior of the building consisted of a single open room. Various hides covered the ground, most of them reptilian, though a few orgok furs broke the pattern. A brazier of khalati claws sat in the center of the room, lighting it with a gentle fire. A hole in the center of the domed ceiling released the resulting smoke.

At one end of the room, on a simple stone bench, sat an elderly orc. His stature dwarfed the humans before him, but his skin hung loose, hinting that he was once even larger than the hulking, one-eyed orc who escorted them inside. Tattoos covered his skin, so many that they blended with one another, leaving him almost white as ivory, with little of his flesh remaining crimson. The crown of his head was bald, but long, flowing silver hair cascaded from the back of his head and over his shoulders.

He squinted and leaned forward as the strangers approached, as if straining to see them, then looked up to the one-eyed warrior. "Forgog, my loyal friend, who stands before me?"

Their escort kneeled and placed a fist over his chest. "Chieftain Garnok, I bring before you the three warriors who hunted us from the sandwalker's camp."

Garnok tilted his head to the side. "I see two humans. Where is the third?"

"I stand among them," Khag said, then also kneeled. "I am Khag of the Flying Serpent Clan, and friend to the humans who stand before you."

The elder sat back with a frown. "The Flying Serpent Clan are no friends to humans, and their clanhome lies far to the south. How came you to be among these northlings?"

"Bondage, at first. Then fellowship and the bonds of blood. They are my brothers in battle."

Garnok nodded. "As is the tale of many who come to join us in the Broken Cliff Clan. Tell me, Khag of the Flying Serpents: Why did you pursue Forgog's war band?"

Brego took a step forward and said, "Forgog was seen taking my chieftain's son, Timik, from his tent during a raid on our people. We have come to retrieve him."

"Ah." Garnok regarded Brego with a suspicious glare as he stroked his silver locks. "So, you've come to slay us and take back the child, is that it?"

"No," Brego said. "Too much blood was spilled the night of the raid, both of my people and yours. We would prefer that you return the child with no further conflict."

Forgog stood and stepped before Brego. Firelight glinted off the bronze plate on his face while his remaining eye bored into Brego's own. "And what of the men I sent to stop you? Did you only talk to them? Why have they not returned?"

Apa snorted. "That's hardly a fair question. You sent them to attack us. They charged with weapons drawn and a pack of skisnik already salivating at the thought of a fresh kill."

"It is a fair question," Garnok said. "What became of them?"

Khag shook his head. "It is regrettable that all but one lay slain. What else were we to do but defend ourselves?"

"All but one?" Forgog asked.

"Yes," Brego said. "We questioned him, then left him to attend to his fallen comrades."

Forgog squinted his one eye, again seeming to peer into the depths of Brego's soul, perhaps searching for some sign of truth or falsehood. "Why would you do this?"

"What need have we to kill him once he was alone and unarmed? He was no threat. Also, it was only right to allow him to aid the dead in their passage to the afterlife."

Forgog snorted, seeming unconvinced. "And I suppose you did the same for those left behind in your camp?"

"In fact," Khag said, "I sent those fallen warriors to Ushtok myself, with Apa's aid." He nodded to the Cressian beside him.

The one-eyed orc turned and glared at the magi. "And how am I supposed to believe you? I should just take your wo—"

"Enough, Forgog," Garnok barked, then turned back to Brego. "If you truly wished only to talk, then the death of those sent to stop you is unfortunate, and there is no undoing this now. I will hear what you have to say."

Brego and Apa shared a glance, then looked at Khag. The red orc nodded, then said, "Great Chieftain, as my friend has said, we come to beg for the return of the child."

"Impossible," Garnok said without hesitation. "If you questioned the warrior you spared, surely you know the child is dangerous. You should know the words of the prophecy: 'When a dohathnik kneels to the sandwalkers, the worldbreaker will be found hiding as a child in the home of their chieftain.' He cannot be allowed to live, for the sake of all our peoples."

Brego let out a long sigh. He knew all too well how hard it was to argue against such deep-seated beliefs. "Just because Khag stood by my side as I sought my people? Surely others of your kind have taken up with Taerwyn tribes before."

"No," Garnok said, "they have not."

"How can you be so sure?" Apa asked. "You allow

those not of your kith to live among you. Is it so hard to believe that one of your people might choose to live with the Taerwyn without being part of some prophecy?"

Forgog's brows knit together at this, then he looked up at the chieftain. "They make a fair point, Garnok. Perhaps we should not be too hasty."

Brego's eyes widened in surprise. He had not expected to find a sympathetic ear in the orcish camp.

Garnok glared at Forgog, silencing the one-eyed warrior without a word. "Because *he* is the first," Garnok said, pointing to Khag. "It is our duty to send the worldbreaker to the afterlife before he can do any harm." The chieftain turned to Brego. "Since you are here, we shall return his body to you after the ritual so you can return him to his people. Like you did for our fallen warriors, we shall allow him the opportunity to pass to the afterlife of the sandwalkers."

Brego twisted his wrists, struggling at the bonds securing them behind his back. Apa must have noticed this, because he met the nomad's eyes and shook his head. Then, the Cressian looked up to Garnok and said, "Great Chieftain, if that is your decision, then I must also bring you a dire warning."

Garnok arced an eyebrow and tilted his head to the side. "And what warning would this be?"

"In two days' time, if we do not return with the child, a great army of the Taerwyn tribes will descend upon the Red Wastes in retribution for the abduction of Timik."

"Oh," Garnok said, "you *will* return with him."

Brego's mouth hung agape. The chieftain had seemed adamant about the sacrifice.

Garnok leaned forward. "After the ritual under tomorrow's moon, his body will be given to you, as I've promised, and you may return him to his people."

The Taerwyn nomad let out a long sigh. "If Timik does not walk by our side when his father's army arrives, I fear it will mean war between our people for the first time in a century."

Forgog's eye shot between Brego and the chieftain. Fear, or perhaps a dire concern, painted the burly warrior's face.

"Then," Garnok said, "there will be war. I wish not for bloodshed, but it will be far less than what the worldbreaker would draw."

Chapter Nine

After their audience, Forgog escorted Brego, Apa, and Khag to a nearby bone cage. The structure was so low they had to hunch over to enter, and it barely provided enough room for the three of them to sit. Even with the overhanging canopies of the village, nightfall was a welcome blessing. The Grashni provided food and water for them, and Forgog assured them that once the ritual was completed on the next night, they would be released.

"We cannot wait until tomorrow night," Apa

whispered once they were alone. "We must make our escape."

Brego examined the hide lashings holding the bones of the cage together. "It should be a simple matter for you to burn through these."

Apa shook his head. "With no fire nearby and without the warmth of the suns, I cannot draw enough heat. We would have to make our escape during the day."

"Without the cover of darkness, that would become a slaughter." Brego tugged at one of the hide strips, but it was bound too tightly to pull apart.

Khag likewise tested their prison, to no avail. He let out a deep huff and sat back. "Brego is right. There will be too many eyes on us during the day. The attempt would likely end in our deaths, and even if we were successful, many Grashni dead would lie in our footsteps."

"What of this prophecy?" Brego asked, looking to Khag. "Do you believe there is any truth to it?"

The red orc let out a long sigh. "My people believe it is a prophecy of the end times, that the worldbreaker will destroy all life in the world. The words are old beyond memory."

"But..." Brego fixed him with a steady gaze, "do *you* believe it?"

Khag shrugged. "It is spoken of, or even thought of, rarely. Like many legends, it lies in the back of one's mind until something inspires thought on it. I never considered it much. I definitely never thought to be a *part* of it. To think that I am the dohathnik mentioned in the prophecy boggles the mind. It seems as if it cannot be true, only because I cannot believe my friendship with you to be its impetus. How could such evil come from something so simple as us having met?"

Brego nodded, then asked, "What do you make of it, Apa?"

The magi twirled his mustache, likely lost deep in thought, for several moments. "Most legends," he finally said, "hold some grain of truth. However, their meaning can be misinterpreted or exaggerated over the years and centuries that follow the original telling. There might be something to it, but it might also be no more than a cautionary tale to teach young orclings to avoid the dangers of the outside world."

"Would you say your people used it as such?" Brego asked Khag.

The red orc shook his head. "No, not necessarily. When I was young, it seemed more a fanciful tale. Also, when the legend was formed, our peoples were likely in constant strife. It would have been unthinkable then that a Grashni would walk with the Taerwyn. Thus, the dohathnik kneeling to the sandwalkers would have indeed been a momentous occurrence."

Just then, Khag cocked his head to the side and peered into the darkness. "Someone comes."

Soft footsteps approached their prison and a large, hulking shadow emerged in the faint moonlight streaming between the canopies overhead. Moonbeams glinted off a bronze plate strapped across one side of the figure's face, the first hint that Forgog had come to visit them.

"I would have words with you," the Grashni warrior said.

The three prisoners exchanged curious glances, and it was Apa who finally responded. "Have your words, then. You have, it seems, a *captive* audience."

Forgog grunted, seeming to make no effort to hide his mirth at the Cressian's jest. "The warrior you spared in the desert has returned and told the same tale of the encounter that you have. I come to give my thanks for sparing his life and allowing him to perform ulukai for the fallen."

"Uluk-who?" Apa asked.

"The rites for the fallen," Khag explained, "as you aided me with after the battle at the Taerwyn camp."

The Cressian nodded. "Ah, yes. My apologies, Forgog. Friend Khag explained the process but did not share the name."

The one-eyed warrior lowered his head in a slight bow. "No offense was taken." He looked back up, meeting the eyes of each prisoner in turn. He looked as if he were contemplating something or wished to say more. He looked away suddenly and let out a long, low breath.

Khag turned as much as he could in the confines of the cage to face his distant Grashni kin. "What is it? Something troubles you."

Forgog looked back, his mouth set in a determined line that only exposed his jutting tusks further. "Is it true war comes to my home in a day's time? Will the sandwalkers enter the stonelands and hunt us down in retribution for the child's death?"

Brego frowned, sorrow and desperation mixing in his gut like a sandstorm. "Though it is the last thing I wish to happen, I cannot tell you otherwise. I have no doubt that should Timik not survive tomorrow night, war between our people will be unavoidable. The Red Wastes will be painted bright crimson with the blood of many from both sides."

Forgog looked away again, staring off into the night.

"You doubt the prophecy," Apa said, clutching at the bone railing of the cage. "You can prevent this madness, you know. Help us, and we can stop any further bloodshed."

"I cannot," Forgog said, turning back. "To go against the wishes of my chieftain, against the words of the elders and the ancestors, is unthinkable."

"And allowing an innocent child to be sacrificed is not?" Brego asked. "What if it were your son, Forgog? What if it were…" The nomad searched his memory for the mention of the child's name. "What if it were Thurog who was to be put to death based on words spoken a thousand years ago? What would you do then?"

Forgog stared at the Taerwyn long and hard, his brows knitted together as he considered the words.

"He is right," Khag said. "Brother, we should not be slaves to the words of the past. The child has done no wrong. How could such a frail thing possibly end all life? The prophecy makes no sense. And, Garnok thinks Timik is the worldbreaker only because I joined the Taerwyn."

Forgog turned his gaze to Khag. "How did it come to be?"

"What?"

"How did you come to kneel at the feet of the Taerwyn chieftain?"

"Well," Apa interjected, "for starters, he never kneeled at his feet. Neither did I. We simply… were accepted."

Forgog nodded to the Cressian, but turned his attention back to Khag. "How did you come to be there? Tell me."

Khag sat back against the bars of the cage and let out a long, low sigh. "As I said, a merchant freed me. It was in Khala, a city far from here. He employed me as his bodyguard. For many cycles of the moon, we were befriended to Apa, the local blacksmith," Khag stopped and nodded to the magi sitting across the cage from him, "who was there hiding from an unsavory past of his own. Then, one day, an escaped Taerwyn slave arrived in town," Khag nodded to Brego, "and was aided by the very same blacksmith. Trouble soon came for them, though, and they fled to Mashim's home for aid. From there, we four fled Khala, but were soon captured and sent to the fighting pit in Cressus. There, we made our escape, although Mashim did not survive the experience."

Khag breathed another long sigh and rubbed at his eyes. Apa and Brego shared sad glances, then all three turned to their captor.

Forgog regarded them long and hard, as if weighing their words. "You three truly are bound by blood then, both spilled and lost."

"We are," Brego said. "After this, my brothers helped me find my long-lost people in the Great Sand Sea. There, those of my kith but not of my kin took me in as if I were family, and upon my word, they accepted Apa and Khag as if they were the same."

"And they never took issue with a Grashni walking

among them?" Forgog asked.

"No," Brego said, then reconsidered. "Well, not until the night you raided our camp. After that, the tribe was near to tearing Khag apart as punishment for the actions of those he resembled."

"And how did you avoid this?" Forgog asked, turning to Khag.

Khag met the large warrior's interrogating eye. "Brego advocated for tolerance, and I promised the chieftain that I would attempt to return his son."

"And, despite the prophecy," Forgog asked, "you would keep this promise?"

"Even if it were true," Khag said. "I gave my word, and I will not break that vow."

"We all gave the same vow," Apa added.

"And we will keep it," Brego said. "With aid or no, we will find a way to free ourselves and save the child. We do this not only for his sake, but to prevent more bloodshed. To prevent the death of more Taerwyn and Grashni alike."

Forgog let out a sharp huff, then drew a long, wickedly jagged obsidian dagger from his belt. "Then I only see one option before me."

The three captives shrank back in the cage, though they could hardly move more than a hand's span from the bones separating them from the orc warrior. Forgog raised the blade with a look of determination in his eye that would not be dissuaded, then brought it down in a swift, powerful stroke. The ebony blade slashed through its target, slicing open the lashings holding the cage closed, and the bone door rattled to the stony ground.

Chapter Ten

Forgog waved them from the cage with an urgent gesture. "Quickly, before I regain my senses."

Brego and Apa surged past the large orc. Khag stopped after stepping from their prison and laid a hand on Forgog's shoulder. "Thank you, brother. You have done the right thing this night."

"Let us *all* hope you are correct," the one-eyed orc replied.

Brego turned, his eyes darting around the darkened corner of the village. "Which way?"

Forgog nodded and jerked his thumb over his shoulder. "He's not far. Follow me." With that, he led the others between several small, round stone huts. He stopped before one such structure, this one smaller than the others and with no windows. While the entrances to most of the huts were open or covered by simple flaps, another bone cage door was lashed over this one's only opening.

Brego stepped forward and held a hand out toward the large orc, palm up. "It would be best if he saw me first."

Forgog nodded and handed his obsidian knife over.

The Taerwyn nomad slashed at the lashings holding the door closed and pulled it away. Inside, the small structure bore only a simple pallet of blankets, atop which laid a small, unmoving form. A lump rose to Brego's throat as he wondered for a moment that they might have been too late. Just as he was about to surge forward in panic, the small form let out a long whine and rolled over.

"Timik," Brego said as he kneeled beside the chieftain's son. "Timik, we are here to bring you home."

The boy's eyelids fluttered open, and he looked up. His face was a mask of confusion at first, then one of astonishment. "Brego?"

The warrior held a finger over his lips. "Quiet, now. We're getting out of here, but you must be swift and silent. Can you do that?"

Timik nodded.

"Can you walk? Are you well?"

The boy nodded again, then rolled over, rose to his knees, and climbed to his feet. "They haven't hurt me. They also fed me and gave me water."

"Good," Brego said, then ushered the boy outside.

Khag and Apa were waiting near the door when the boy emerged, and Timik nearly squealed in joy upon seeing them. He ran to Apa and hugged the magi, but he cast a wary glance at Khag.

The red orc nodded to the boy with sadness in his eyes.

Apa looked to his friend and said, "It will take time. He had a fright."

"This is touching," Brego said as he emerged behind the boy, "but we need to be going. Forgog, what would be the best way to escape the village?"

Timik cocked his head to the side, likely confused at hearing a name he did not recognize and only seeing the three familiar figures nearby.

The one-eyed warrior stepped from the shadows between two nearby huts. "Our best chance is to skirt the edge of the canyon until we come to the fissure, then you simply return the way you came."

"Oh, *simply*?" Apa moaned. "Those crevices were like a maze. Had we not been following the drake's tracks, we never would have found you."

"It seems as such upon first glance, but it's not as complicated as it seems," Forgog said. "Many of the paths split and then meet one another. If you always turn east, you'll find the exit."

"Very well," Brego said. "Let's go."

Forgog turned to Timik, who was at this point clutching Apa's robes and trembling as if he's seen a ghost. "I hope you may one day forgive me," the large orc said. Moonlight glinted on the brass plate over his missing eye.

Timik screamed.

"What in the blazes?" Apa barked as the boy ran behind him, still clutching his clothes.

Brego stepped over and kneeled beside the magi, gently gripped Timik's arm, and pulled him from his hiding place. "It's okay. Forgog is helping us."

"No," Timik cried. "No, he's the one who took me. He's the one-eyed brute. I won't let him take me again. I won't."

Apa kneeled on the other side of the boy, trying to calm him. "Brego speaks true. He has seen the error of his ways and is helping us."

Khag moved to step forward, but Forgog stretched his arm across the other orc's chest and shook his head.

"Come on," Brego hissed. "We must move with even more haste now. That scream surely roused half the village."

Just as surely as the suns rise in the morning, several groggy-eyed orcs rushed into the small space between the cliffside and the small huts. Most of them were armed, responding to a child screaming at danger as anyone might, rushing to stave off whatever threat presented itself. The shock on their faces when they arrived showed they had not expected to see this strange gathering.

"No!" Timik screamed. With that word, it was like

an invisible force slammed into Forgog and Khag, sending them both hurtling away to slam into the wall of a nearby hut. The boy's back arched suddenly and his arms snapped outright to his sides, then he rose from the ground as if lifted by unseen hands. His feet dragged across the ground below him, then left it as he floated into the air, surrounded by a constellation of floating, swirling stones.

Brego scrambled back, as did Apa. His heart thrummed in his chest as he looked up at the levitating child.

Timik's eyes rolled back until only white was showing. His head tilted back, and he screamed, "They will not take me!"

The assembled orcs charged forward, their weapons raised, only to be met with a storm of flying stones. The projectiles streamed out seemingly of their own accord, striking the oncoming foes with sickening, wet thumps as they pummeled flesh and shattered bones.

Strange words uttered forth from Timik's mouth in a voice that was wholly unlike his own, deep and guttural. "Ganash borok estat! Horevum tilistit!" His back spasmed at the last word, and a dozen fallen orcs closest to him suddenly burst into flames.

Brego's eyes were wide with horror at the sight. His mind reeled as he tried to understand what was happening. Apa, on the other side of the boy from him, looked similarly befuddled. "What is this madness?" Brego called out.

The magi shook his head. "It is as if he's possessed. His words are of an old tongue, one I've not heard spoken outside the Tower of Brass in Cressus."

"How can this be?" Brego shouted as a fresh swarm of stones swirled in the air so rapidly the canyon sounded as if a sandstorm engulfed it.

Apa simply shook his head. "I don't know."

"The worldbreaker!" a deep, gravelly voice cried out from the edge of the clearing. Garnok stepped around the burning bodies to approach them. "I warned you, and you did not listen. Now you have unleashed the worldbreaker, and he will destroy us all!"

Timik's eyes met the old orc's, and the chieftain was flung away without another word.

Khag roused from where he laid in a heap against a hut and surged forward with a primal growl, charging directly at Timik.

"Khag, no!" Brego yelled, but his friend was not listening.

He came within several steps of the boy, but could not press through the whirlwind of stones. Dozens of them buffeted him, pummeling him from head to toe. He tried to press through despite the bloody wounds, then a fist-sized rock slammed into his temple, and he collapsed to the ground, unmoving.

"Khag!" Brego screamed, reaching a desperate hand toward his fallen friend.

"We must do something!" Apa yelled out. He rose to his knees and spread his hands out, palms down, and closed his eyes. Shimmers of heat formed between his palms and the ground as he drew in what warmth remained in the soil and stones. With a shove, he sent a gust of air into the whirlwind of stones. It was too little though, despite being the most the magi could muster in the cold of night. The stones stuttered a moment, but did not fall, and the boy in the center of the storm seemed unaffected.

Timik turned his gaze to Apa, though his eyes remained rolled up and showed no color. He reached out a hand toward the magi, and Apa's breath caught as he too floated above the ground. He struggled against the invisible force bearing him aloft, then shuddered and spasmed as thousands of grains of sand shot forth and swirled around him. Tiny scratches appeared in his flesh as the personal sandstorm flayed him.

"Apa!" Brego called out. He looked down at Khag, who still lay motionless at Timik's feet, blood trickling from a dozen wounds or more. The nomad knew what he had to do, but had not the heart to do it. His fist tightened around the handle of Forgog's obsidian knife, still in his hand from cutting open the boy's prison door.

The boy they'd come all this way to find. The boy they'd ventured into the Red Wastes to rescue. The boy who they'd played and laughed and cried with over the last several moons. The son of the chieftain who'd accepted Brego back into the Taerwyn. Into their home.

Brego looked up at that same boy, who was killing his friend. Apa screamed as the swirling sands ground away layers of flesh.

The ground shook and rumbled beneath Brego. Large stones, larger than horses, broke from the cliffs and tumbled into the village, crushing buildings beneath them. The wood and bone structures that ran the cliff walls shook and collapsed, tumbling to the canyon floor alongside the stones. Screams of panic and pain rang out from across the entire chasm as orc and human alike fled for their lives or loss them in the tumult.

"Stop him!" Garnok yelled out.

Brego turned. The old orc chieftain stumbled closer, supported by a Grashni warrior on one side and a Taerwyn refugee on the other. Blood ran from the corner of his mouth. One eye was swollen shut and black bruises obscured many of the white tattoos covering his face. "You must stop him," the chieftain urged again, "or the world itself will break!"

As further proof of prescience, the ground beneath their feet rumbled. Long, deep crevices cracked open beneath the village, swallowing stone huts whole and sending fleeing villagers plummeting into an unseeable abyss.

Timik turned to the elderly orc. His attention diverted, the sandstorm engulfing Apa relented, and the magi collapsed to the ground. Brego could not tell if he was breathing, but his skin was covered in abrasions and so much blood stained his tattered robes that it would have surprised the nomad if his friend still lived.

"Stop this!" Garnok cried out as a similar storm of sand rose around him.

The canyon rumbled again, and the central pillar of stone shuddered. It swayed from side to side and seemed it could fall at any moment. Clouds obscured the moon and thunder crashed in the sky. Lightning streamed down in bright flashes, and several homes in the village exploded in great torrents of fire, sending debris flying in every direction.

Garnok opened his mouth again, but only a scream of pain issued forth.

His heart thrumming against his ribs, Brego knew what must be done. He did not understand what was happening, or how they could have been wrong, but it was clear he needed to act. While Timik's attention was on Garnok, Brego stood and surged forward.

The whirlwind of stones surrounding the floating boy slammed into Brego as he advanced. He held an arm over his face to shield it. He had born the lash of the slaver's whip, the bite of hammer and blade in the fighting pits, and beatings in the stone quarries of Shem. Brego was no stranger to pain, so he strode through this storm of anguish as he had waded through similar torrents almost all his life.

When he was but a single pace from Timik, the boy turned in the air to face him. His eyes were wide and lifeless, seeing all and unseeing, as his face turned to the nomad. Brego met those blank eyes for only a moment before plunging the obsidian blade into Timik's chest with both hands, pressing forward until the bone handle pressed against the boy's sternum.

And in a moment, it was over.

The ground stopped shaking, the thunder faded into the distance, and the storm of stones fell crashing to the ground with a deafening rattle. A moment later, whatever force held Timik aloft released him, and he fell limp into Brego's arms.

The boy blinked and looked up with his pupils wide. "Brego?"

Tears filled the warrior's eyes as he looked down at the boy. "I'm here."

"I'm scared," Timik said as tears welled up in his eyes and rolled down his cheeks. "There was something in me."

"It's gone now," Brego said as he stroked the boy's unruly hair back from his face.

"It hurts," Timik moaned, then coughed, blood speckling his lips and running down his chin.

"Timik, I'm sor—"

"No," the boy said, cutting him off. "Thank you for freeing me."

Chapter Eleven

Ora and Aporo rose to cast their light over a devastated village. Plumes of smoke from smoldering fires rose beyond the canyon walls. Wails of grief and sobs of mourning echoed from the red stones as the survivors performed the final rites for the fallen.

By the setting of Ora, under the orange glow of Aporo, three figures emerged from a narrow slit in the stone bluffs. They shuffled away from the battered village and to the north, to face another storm.

Brego, Apa, and Khag stopped as Aporo neared the

horizon. The village healers had tended to all three, bandaging their wounds with salves. Apa bore the worst of them all and was covered from head to toe with linen wrappings, with only his eyes and blistered lips exposed to the desert heat.

Khag lowered a burden bundled in hide blankets from his shoulder and laid it reverently upon the ground before them.

Brego looked down at the still figure with tears in his eyes.

"If you shed many more, you'll have no water left within you," Apa said as he laid a hand on his friend's shoulder.

"Let it flow, then," Brego said, "so I might die and be relieved of my guilt."

"We have need of you yet," Khag grumbled. "Look."

On the horizon, over the first dunes of the Great Sand Sea, dozens of silhouettes on horseback emerged. Then, hundreds. They rode down the dune at a gallop and drew up to a halt before the three.

Chieftain Raniq rode to the fore of the army and pulled his horse to an uneasy halt. He looked over the three battered figures before him, then his eyes fell to the bundle at their feet. They grew wide, and he leaped from his mount. "What is this? Where is my son?"

Brego took a deep breath and stepped forward. "I'm sorry, Raniq. Timik has fallen."

The chieftain looked down at the bundle again, then fell to his knees before it. He laid his hands upon the still form of his son's body and wailed in grief.

Brego neared to within a hand's breath of Raniq. "There was more to this than we expected. This is as it had to be. Timik was host to some foul demon. He killed many in the village, and we believe would have broken the entire world had he not been set free from his bonds."

Raniq's body shook with rage as his eyes met Brego's. "Surely, there is witchcraft at work here. They have poisoned your mind. Come, stand by my side in battle. Help me to avenge my son."

Brego lowered his eyes. "That, I cannot do. I cannot avenge a deed I committed with my own hands.

The revelation seemed to strike Raniq as surely as a sword thrust through his gut. His eyes grew wide, and his knuckles whitened as he clenched the hilt of the sword at his side. "No..." He shook his head as if to drive away this impossible news. "Madness!" he yelled. His eyes darted between the three men standing before him. "Apa of Cressus and Khag of the Grashni, you have both proven yourself friends to the Taerwyn. Will you not stand by us now and reaffirm that bond?"

"I cannot," Apa said. "The Grashni only did what was needed to preserve life, both of their own people and those beyond the borders of their homes, including those of your own people."

Raniq's rage seemed ready to overtake his grief as his eyes narrowed and he glared at Khag. "And you?"

The red orc stood tall, squaring his shoulders. "I regret I cannot assuage your grief, Chieftain Raniq. I respect you and loved your son, but the Grashni have done only what the fates demanded of them."

The Taerwyn warriors gathered behind Raniq seemed to grow restless. The time for talk was nearing its end, but the chieftain seemed to wish one last chance to turn Brego's course, to whom his gaze then fell. "And what of your people? What of the blood shared between us?"

Brego took a step forward and spread his arms wide, gesturing to the man standing on either side of him. "I stand by my decision, and I stand by my brothers. The blood I have shed with them means more to me than the blood I share with you."

Raniq, suddenly calm as the eye of a sandstorm, took a deep breath and said, "Then, it is war, and you have chosen to die with the enemy."

"There is no need for war," Brego said as he lowered his hands and took another step forward. "There is no need for more bloodshed. Search my eyes, my chieftain. Tell me truly that you see madness, or witchcraft, or malice. You trusted me. You trusted all three of us. Tell me now you no longer trust us."

The chieftain stared into Brego's eyes, the moment drawing out in the silence of the stony wastes. Not a soul dared to utter a sound to disturb that silence.

Finally, Raniq spoke. "I cannot. I cannot see those things, Brego. I see only iron determination and sorrow."

"Then go," Brego said. "Go, all of you, and return to the sands. Return to your people in peace and in good health. Do not die today for vengeance. Do not die to sate your anger. Do not lead your people to ruin, Raniq, for they will find only ruin upon these stones."

Raniq glared hard at Brego, then looked him over, likely seeing the freshly bandaged wounds covering his body for the first time. Then his eyes turned to Khag, then lingered long on the pitiful form of Apa.

Inferring the unspoken question, Brego said, "Timik did all this, and worse. We were among the lucky few to survive the onslaught of whatever demon possessed him. Had I not ended his attack, surely the same fate would have befallen all of you, and more, in time."

"You say he was possessed?" Raniq asked, bewilderment replacing the anger on his face.

Brego nodded. "The Grashni prophesied long ago that a Taerwyn boy would destroy the world. The worldbreaker, they called him."

Apa stepped forward. "It was Timik's poor fortune that he was destined to be the worldbreaker, host to some dark force. He uttered words in an ancient, dark language forbidden to be spoken even among the Magi outside the walls of the Tower of Brass in Cressus. An ancient evil overcame him. He was a slave to this evil, and only in death could he be freed."

"And you believe this?" Raniq asked, turning back to Brego.

"We saw with our own eyes when the demon took hold of him," Brego said.

Apa unwound the bandages covering his face, revealing flesh ground bare, red, and raw by the sandstorm with which Timik assailed him the night before. "And we felt its fury with our own flesh."

Raniq drew back in horror, then looked over Brego and Khag, again appraising the bandages covering much of their bodies as well.

"It had to be done," Brego said.

"And you did this… with your own hand?" Raniq asked, his eyes again meeting Brego's.

The nomad nodded. "I did what had to be done."

Wind whistled through the wastes between the buttes and plateaus. Sand swirled around them, gathering around their ankles a moment before blowing out toward the Great Sand Sea. As if drawn by this wind as much as he was swayed by Brego's argument, Raniq nodded. "I will take my son's body back to the sands, and on to Kabinai. However, I cannot welcome the slayer of my son back into my tent." His voice rose so all could hear his next words. "You, Brego, are no longer welcome with the Taerwyn. Warriors gathered here from a dozen tribes will ride out with these words. None of the peoples of the sand will ever welcome you into their tents. Though you may have done what was necessary, our law is that no man shall harm a child, no matter what. I forgive you, but I cannot undo the law. You are Taerwyn no longer."

* * *

Ora was high overhead by the time Brego, Apa, and Khag returned to the Grashni village. The tribe was already hard at work clearing the debris of ruined homes to start the process of rebuilding.

Garnok limped toward the three, leaning heavily on a long staff. "You have returned."

Khag stepped forward and placed a fist over his chest. "With happy news on a sad day, Chieftain. The sandwalkers return to the Great Sand Sea. There will be no war."

"This is indeed happy news," Garnok said. "You

have my thanks for this, and…" he turned sad eyes on Brego, "for ending the worldbreaker. Though you may have been misguided in freeing him and preventing the ritual, I cannot condemn you for your beliefs and loyalties, just as I asked you to be understanding of our beliefs. The boy was not overcome until our warriors surrounded him." Garnok let out a long, sad sigh. "Perhaps the prophecy was a self-fulfilling one. The boy's fear of the Grashni unleashed the worldbreaker, and he feared us only because we took him in response to the prophecy. Maybe if we had left him be…"

Brego shook his head. "If terror is what unleashed the demon, it would have come in time, regardless. No one lives a life devoid of fear. The day would have come, one way or the other."

"You are wise, Brego of the sandwalkers."

The nomad cast his eyes down. "I am no longer of the sandwalkers."

The old orc cocked his head to the side. "You are not returning with them? With your people?"

The nomad warrior looked at Apa and Khag in turn, then back to Garnok. "I am with my people now."

The chieftain nodded and waved for them to follow

him as he turned and hobbled back toward the central stone pillar. "Many among us know what it is like to be without a home. You saved us from the worldbreaker. You might yet find a home here."

Brego looked around the village. The weight of accusatory eyes bearing down on the three of them was too heavy to ignore. "We caused the devastation here. Had we but listened to your words and let you carry out the sacrifice, many who perished last night would still be alive."

"How many more would have perished if the sandwalkers brought war to the stonelands? By unleashing the worldbreaker for a short time, you have proven the prophecy and justified our actions. This may be all that stood between us and ruin. And, who among us is without fault?" Garnok asked, turning back to look at Brego. "Forgiveness is not given, it is earned. Stay here. *Earn* it. Surely you, Khag, desire to be among your people again."

Khag's eyes returned after a survey of the clan surrounding them. "Not like this. Not today. I fear there is too much grief for us to seek forgiveness. At least, it is too fresh."

Garnok nodded and scratched at the thinning hair on his temple with a long, sharp nail. "Your words are wise for one so young, Khag of the Flying Serpent Clan." He let out a long sigh. "Perhaps you are right. Wherever you go, your journey will be long and difficult. At the very least, tell me what aid I can offer you."

"Mounts, food, and water," Brego said. "With only that, we demand more than we deserve, but it is what we require"

"Nonsense," Garnok said. "If not for you, we'd all be dead."

Brego shook his head again. "If not for us—"

The old orc held up a hand. "Let us argue it no further. You'll have your supplies."

* * *

Brego pulled on the drake's harness to ensure the saddle was steady and the various packs secured to its flanks. A bundle of supplies larger than he could have asked for sat high on the beast's rump. Similar packs adorned another two drakes.

The horse-sized lizard hissed as he yanked the

straps and turned its long neck to the side, squinting a yellow eye to glare at him. It opened its mouth, bearing sharp teeth. Its large hind legs scratched with anticipation at the ground and its long, slender forelimbs wavered near its chest, ready to lash out at any moment with razor-sharp talons.

"I'd rather a horse," Brego muttered, looking the beast in the eye, "but we're simply must learn to tolerate one another."

The drake hissed again, shook its head as if to express its own discontent at the pairing, and turned away.

"It seems we are ready," Apa said as he climbed onto the back of another drake with great caution. Still wrapped from head to toe in bandages, covered in tattered robes, and with a hood drawn over his head, the magi looked more like a shrouded corpse than a man. He winced with every movement, but offered no complaint.

Khag also mounted, seeming more at ease with the serpentine mounts than his human counterparts.

"I thought you preferred to walk," Brego said.

Khag shook his head. "Not so. It is rather that I can't

stand the smell of horse."

"And you think these beasts smell better?"

Leaning forward, Khag ran a tender hand along the drake's long neck. "Don't listen to him. You don't stink, you beautiful creature."

Apa rolled his eyes. "Oh, great. Now he's in love."

Brego shook with laughter, then climbed onto his drake. "Are you sure about this, Khag?"

The red orc nodded. "I have no more a right to homestead here than either of you. And, for as much of the world outside the Red Wastes that I've seen, I'd like to see more of it. I think I've spent too much time among your kind to settle down. Your human desire to spread across the entirety of the world seems to be infectious."

"And you, Apa?" Brego asked. "You could return north."

"To live as a fugitive once again?" the magi asked. "No, I think not."

"So, I suppose that leaves the south," Khag said.

"Yes," Brego said. "Eventually, to the Gemstone Coast. Perhaps there we might find a place to settle."

"But first, we must travel through Heshian lands,"

Apa said, his voice dripping with trepidation.

Brego nodded and dug his heels into the drake's flank. "Onward then, to the Empire of the Scale."

About the Author

B.K. Bass is the author of over a dozen works of science fiction, fantasy, and horror inspired by the pulp fiction magazines of the early 20th century and classic speculative fiction. He is also a freelance editor with experience both as a publisher and editor-in-chief of a literary journal. When B.K. isn't dreaming up new worlds to explore, he spends his time as a lifelong student of history, bookworm, and film buff.

Find out more and connect with B.K. at
https://bkbass.com

Discover more exciting adventures at

BKBASS.COM

www.ingramcontent.com/pod-product-compliance
Lightning Source LLC
LaVergne TN
LVHW090049160826
845672LV00015B/1610

* 9 7 9 8 3 6 5 9 8 5 9 6 4 *